Albert's Old Shoes

Albert's Old Shoes

Story by
Stephen Muir

Illustrations by
Mary Jane Muir

Stoddart Kids

Stoddart Publishing gratefully ackowledges the support of the
Canada Council and the Ontario Arts Council in the development
of writing and publishing in Canada.

First published in 1987 by Scholastic Canada

Published in 1996 by Stoddart Publishing Co. Limited

Published in Canada in 1997 by Stoddart Kids,
a division of Stoddart Publishing Co. Limited
34 Lesmill Road, Toronto, Canada M3B 2T6
Tel: (416) 445-3333 Fax (416) 445-5967
e-mail Customer.Service@ccmailgw.genpub.com

Published in the United States in 1997 by Stoddart Kids
85 River Rock Drive, Suite 202
Buffalo, New York 14207
Toll free 1-800-805-1083
e-mail gdsinc@genpub.com

Canadian Cataloguing in Publication Data

Muir, Stephen
Albert's old shoes

ISBN 0-7737-5777-5

I. Muir, Mary Jane.   II. Title.

PS8576.U364A8 1995   jC813'.54   C95-932489-5
PZ7.M74A1 1995

Printed and bound in Hong Kong by
Book Art Inc., Toronto.

For Shannon
S.M.

For Shannon,
with special thanks to Elizabeth Brochman,
Sue, Bob, Mary, Paul, Deborah, Maryjean and Randy.
M.J.M.

Albert had some plain brown shoes. They were scuffed-up and ugly and old.
He hated them.

At school everyone teased Albert about his shoes.

Actually, most of the time it was only Bill who teased him, but Albert felt so awful he thought it was everyone.

"Hey, Albert!" Bill would shout. "Where'd you get such ugly shoes? They sure look dumb!"

Albert didn't know what to say when Bill bugged him, so he just said nothing.

Every day after school Albert went home and watched TV. He would rather have stayed outside to play with the other kids, but he didn't want to be teased about his ugly, scuffed-up, funny-looking old brown shoes.

"Why don't you go outside, Albert?" his mother would ask.

"I don't want to," Albert would say, although that wasn't really the truth.

"Is something bothering you?" his mother would ask.

"No," Albert would reply firmly. And that would end the conversation.

One day when Albert came home he found a large box on the kitchen table. He wondered if it was for him. Albert imagined that inside the box was a pair of brand-new running shoes.

"I hope Mom got me some white running shoes," Albert said to himself. "I hope they're the kind made of leather with red stripes on the sides."

Albert decided he would wear the running shoes to school the next day. Maybe if he had new shoes people wouldn't make fun of him.

Albert could hardly wait to talk to his mother. He just knew she would say, "Guess what I got for you at the store, Albert?" and he would say, "New running shoes!" and his mom would say, "Yes!"

So when his mom came into the kitchen and said, "Guess what I got for you at the store today, Albert?" Albert said, "New running shoes!"

But instead of saying "Yes!" his mother said, "Silly boy! I didn't get you running shoes. I bought you a nice new bedspread!" And she pulled it out of the box to show him.

Albert couldn't believe his eyes.

"Mom," he said, "why in the world would you buy me a dumb bedspread?"

"Albert! Don't talk to me like that!" said his mother.

"I'm sorry, Mom," said Albert. "It's a very nice bedspread. Thank you very much."

But Albert didn't really like the bedspread at all.

The next morning Albert was still angry with his mom and angry with his shoes and angry with the whole world.

"I hate these stupid old shoes," Albert thought to himself as he got dressed.

"I hate these scuffed-up, stupid old shoes," Albert muttered as he marched off to school.

"I hate these funny-looking, scuffed-up, stupid old shoes," Albert grumbled out loud as he entered the schoolyard.

"I hate these funny-looking, scuffed-up, stupid old ugly brown shoes!" he yelled as he watched the other kids playing. Albert saw the soccer ball rolling toward him. He was so mad that he ran and kicked it as hard as he possibly could.

Everyone in the schoolyard stopped what they were doing and stared. They weren't looking at Albert, though. They were looking at the soccer ball.

It was soaring higher than anyone had ever kicked a soccer ball before. It arched up into the sky like a rocket, sailing right over the two-story school.

"Wow!" someone said.

"Fantastic!" said another.

"Incredible!" said someone else.

Then Bill walked over to Albert. But this time Bill didn't tease him.

"That was some kick," said Bill.

"Thanks," Albert replied.

"What kind of shoes are you wearing?" asked Bill.

"Oh, just my old brown shoes," Albert said.

"Hmph," said Bill. "Want to play soccer with us after school?"

Albert pretended not to be too interested. "Okay," he said.

That afternoon Albert ran all the way home. He wanted to get to the soccer field as soon as he could.

When he went into the kitchen he noticed another box on the table. But he was in such a hurry, he didn't pay much attention. Besides, he thought to himself, it's probably something really dumb like a shower curtain.

"What's the big rush, Albert?" asked his mom.

"I'm going to play soccer," said Albert.

"Don't you want to see what's in the box first?" his mother asked.

Albert was annoyed that she was keeping him waiting just to show him a shower curtain.

"It's a very nice shower curtain," said Albert. "I have to go."

"Silly boy! This isn't a shower curtain," his mother said.

"Mom! I've got to go or I'll miss the game," Albert said impatiently. "I give up. What's in the box?"

"Come and see," said his mother, as she took off the lid.

Albert rushed over to the box. He was going to have a quick look, say "That's nice" and hurry to the park. But when he looked inside he couldn't believe his eyes. There, nestled in the wrapping paper, was a brand new pair of white leather running shoes with blue stripes on the sides.

"New running shoes!" Albert shouted.

Albert put on his new shoes and ran all the way to the park. He couldn't wait to show the other kids. But when he got there, he noticed something very odd.

For the third time that day Albert couldn't believe his eyes.

Everyone was wearing ugly, scuffed-up, funny-looking, old brown shoes.

Exactly like the ones he was wearing when he kicked the soccer ball over the school that morning.

Everyone was trying to be just like him!

Albert started to smile. Then he started to giggle. And then he started laughing right out loud.

When the other kids saw what Albert was laughing about, they started giggling too.

Soon the whole park was full of people giggling and laughing and shouting and having fun. And Albert was in the middle of them, having the most fun of all.

The End.